NO MORE MONKEYS

Retold by STEVEN ANDERSON

Illustrated by DOREEN MARTS

CANTATA
LEARNING

MANKATO, MINNESOTA

WWW.CANTATALEARNING.COM

**CANTATA
LEARNING**

MANKATO, MINNESOTA

Published by Cantata Learning
1710 Roe Crest Drive
North Mankato, MN 56003
www.cantatalearning.com

Library of Congress Control Number: 2014957025
978-1-63290-279-5 (hardcover/CD)
978-1-63290-431-7 (paperback/CD)
978-1-63290-473-7 (paperback)

No More Monkeys by Steven Anderson
Illustrated by Doreen Marts

Book design, Tim Palin Creative
Editorial direction, Flat Sole Studio
Executive musical production and direction, Elizabeth Draper
Music arranged and produced by Steven C Music

Printed in the United States of America.

VISIT
WWW.CANTATALEARNING.COM/ACCESS-OUR-MUSIC
TO SING ALONG TO THE SONG

Monkeys are known for their jumping and swinging **abilities**. But what if monkeys lived in your house? What kind of **mischief** would they make?

Now turn the page, and sing along.

Five little monkeys
jumping on the bed.
One fell off and
bumped her head.

Mama called the **doctor**,
and the doctor said,
"No more monkeys
jumping on the bed!"

Four little monkeys jumping on the bed.

One fell off and bumped his head.

Mama called the doctor, and the doctor said,

"No more monkeys jumping on the bed!"

Three little monkeys jumping on the bed.

One fell off and bumped her head.

Mama called the doctor, and the doctor said,

"No more monkeys jumping on the bed!"

11

Can you jump and **dance** like a monkey?

Now really dance like a crazy monkey!

Two little monkeys
jumping on the bed.
One fell off and
bumped his head.

Mama called the doctor,
and the doctor said,
"No more monkeys
jumping on the bed!"

One little monkey jumping on the bed.

One fell off and bumped his head.

Mama called the doctor, and the doctor said,
"Put those monkeys to bed!"

Just like the monkeys, it's time for bed!

21

SONG LYRICS
No More Monkeys

Five little monkeys jumping on the bed.
One fell off and bumped her head.

Mama called the doctor, and the
    doctor said,
"No more monkeys jumping on the
    bed!"

Four little monkeys jumping on the
    bed.
One fell off and bumped his head.

Mama called the doctor, and the
    doctor said,
"No more monkeys jumping on the
    bed!"

Three little monkeys jumping on the
    bed.
One fell off and bumped her head.

Mama called the doctor, and the
    doctor said,

"No more monkeys jumping on the
    bed!"

Can you jump and dance
like a monkey?

Now really dance like a crazy monkey!

Two little monkeys jumping on the bed.
One fell off and bumped his head.

Mama called the doctor, and the
    doctor said,
"No more monkeys jumping on the
    bed!"

One little monkey jumping on the bed.
One fell off and bumped his head.

Mama called the doctor, and the
    doctor said,
"Put those monkeys to bed!"

No More Monkeys

Marimba Pop
Steven C Music

1. Five lit - tle mon - keys jump-ing on the bed. One fell off and bumped her head.

Ma - ma called the doc - tor, and the doc - tor said, "No more mon - keys jump-ing on the bed!"

Verse 2
Four little monkeys jumping on the bed.
One fell off and bumped his head.
Mama called the doctor, and the doctor said,
"No more monkeys jumping on the bed!"

Verse 3
Three little monkeys jumping on the bed.
One fell off and bumped her head.
Mama called the doctor, and the doctor said,
"No more monkeys jumping on the bed!"

Verse 4
Two little monkeys jumping on the bed.
One fell off and bumped his head.
Mama called the doctor, and the doctor said,
"No more monkeys jumping on the bed!"

Verse 5
One little monkey jumping on the bed.
One fell off and bumped his head.
Mama called the doctor, and the doctor said,
"Put those monkeys to bed!"

Can you jump and dance like a monkey?

Now really dance like a crazy monkey!

GLOSSARY

abilities—the powers to do something

bumped—to have knocked into something

dance—to move in time to music

doctor—a person who is trained to treat sick or hurt people

mischief—playful behavior that may cause harm to oneself or others

GUIDED READING ACTIVITIES

1. Read this story again and use your hands to count how many monkeys are jumping on the bed. Before you turn the page, guess how many monkeys will still be jumping on the bed.

2. Why do you think the mom and doctor don't want the monkeys to jump on the bed?

3. What would you tell the monkeys if you were their mom?

TO LEARN MORE

Dahl, Michael. *Little Monkey Calms Down*. North Mankato, MN: Capstone Picture Window Books, 2014.

Diaz, Joanna Ruelos. *Animals in the Rain Forest*. North Mankato, MN: Capstone Picture Window Books, 2014.

Kralovansky, Susan Holt. *Monkey or Ape?* Minneapolis: ABDO Publishing Company, 2015.

Meister, Cari. *Do You Really Want to Meet a Monkey?* Mankato, MN: Amicus Illustrated, 2015.